First published in Dutch as *Buiten op de boerderij*
By Uitgeverij Ploegsma, Amsterdam
Copyright © *Buiten op de boerderij* by Nannie Kuiper
& Alex de Wolf, Uitgeverij Ploegsma, 2006, Amsterdam
English version © Floris Books, Edinburgh 2012

British Library CIP Data available
ISBN 978-086315-858-2
Printed in Singapore

Reuben and Barney's Day on the Farm

Nannie Kuiper & Alex de Wolf

Floris Books

Reuben wakes up and says hello to Barney.
Woof! says Barney. He's ready to start their day on the farm.

Outside, the chickens are hungry. *Cluck, cluck*, they say.
The rooster runs for his breakfast.

Reuben gives them water. Barney is thirsty too.

One of the chickens runs away, so Reuben tries to catch it with a lasso.

They give the rabbits carrots for breakfast, and Reuben has a cuddle.
But Barney is hungry too.

Maybe Barney would like some strawberries?
Woof! He's not so sure.

Next, they pull out the weeds in the vegetable patch.
Barney loves digging!

Then they find the goats in the flowerbed, and chase them away.
Baaaaaa! say the naughty goats.

Reuben gives the pigs some apples. *Oink, oink*, they say.
They love apples, and so does Reuben.

Today, the beekeeper is collecting honey. *Bzzzz, bzzzz!* say all the buzzy bees.
Don't get too close, Barney!

Now it's time to play. Reuben jumps into the hay. Will Barney jump in too?

Reuben and Barney are tired after their busy morning.
They go to sleep under the apple tree.

Now it's time to visit Reuben's favourite animal. On the way, Barney finds a bird's nest in the hedge, but the birds have flown away.

Reuben's favourite animal is Chestnut, the pony. *Neeeeiiiiiiigh!* They gallop out to the fields to find Dad. Barney runs to keep up.

Reuben's dad is digging up potatoes with his tractor. "Come and help," he says.
But Barney wants to play.

They run to the stream. Reuben takes a big jump, but Barney likes to get wet.

They say hello to the cows, and the cows say, *Mooooooooo!*
Their udders are full of milk.

"Leave those cowpats, Barney. They help to make the grass grow."

Now the farmers are harvesting grain, and making big bales of straw.

Birds flock to the field to eat the leftover grain. Reuben tries to count them:
"One... ten... a hundred... maybe more."

It's nearly time to go home, but they stop at the orchard for a bucket of pears.
It's getting windy now.

In the distance Reuben sees a windmill. Its sails are turning in the wind.

Soon they are back at the farmyard, where Dad is sawing logs.
"It's time for supper," he says. "You've had a busy day."

Reuben and Barney wave goodbye to all the animals.
They've had a wonderful day on the farm.